BOOKS BY TESS GALLAGHER

STEPPING OUTSIDE   1974
INSTRUCTIONS TO THE DOUBLE   1976
UNDER STARS   1977
ON YOUR OWN   1978
PORTABLE KISSES   1978
WILLINGLY   1984

WILLINGLY

POEMS BY

TESS GALLAGHER

GRAYWOLF PRESS
1984

*This publication was supported in part by grants from
the* National Endowment for the Arts *and the* Washington
State Arts Commission. *The author wishes to thank the*
John Simon Guggenheim Memorial Foundation, Syracuse University,
and the National Endowment for the Arts *for their support
during the writing of these poems.*

GRATEFUL ACKNOWLEDGMENT IS DUE
THE EDITORS OF THE FOLLOWING PERIODICALS
IN WHICH MANY OF THE POEMS
IN THIS COLLECTION
FIRST APPEARED:
*The American Poetry Review, The Atlantic Monthly, Ironwood,
The Iowa Review, Life Magazine, MS. Magazine, The Ontario
Review, Open Places, The Paris Review, Syracuse
Scholar* and *Vanity Fair.*

"Bird-Window-Flying," "Tableau Vivant," "Gray Eyes" and
"Black Silk" were first published in *The New Yorker.*

ISBN 0–915308–45–2
ISBN 0–915308–46–0 *(paper)*
LC NO. 83–82867

2 4 6 8 9 7 5 3
FIRST PRINTING *1984*

Composed by Wilsted *&* Taylor
Manufactured by Edwards Brothers
Designed by Scott Freutel

Published by Graywolf Press
POST OFFICE BOX 142
PORT TOWNSEND, WASHINGTON
98368

for RAYMOND CARVER

CONTENTS

I

3   Sudden Journey

4   Bird Window Flying

6   Unsteady Yellow

7   Not There

8   Black Ships

10   Linoleum

13   In That Time When It Was Not the Fashion

16   The Shirts

18   Painted Steps

19   You Talk on Your Telephone; I Talk on Mine

22   Conversation with a Fireman from Brooklyn

23   Crêpes Flambeau

25   I Save Your Coat, but You Lose It Later

II

29   What Cathál Said

30   3 A.M. Kitchen: My Father Talking

32   Boat Ride

39   Accomplishment

41   Black Silk

42 *Candle, Lamp & Firefly*

44 *The Kneeling One*

46 *Devotion: That It Flow;*
That There Be Concentration

52 *View from an Empty Chair*

54 *I Take Care of You;*
A Lantern Dashes by in the Grass

56 *Willingly*

58 *Stopping Place*

59 *Some with Wings, Some with Manes*

61 *Some Painful Butterflies Pass Through*

63 *Eating the Sparrows*

III

67 *Skylights*

68 *Tableau Vivant*

70 *The Hug*

72 *Reading Aloud*

75 *Unanswered Letter*

77 *Each Bird Walking*

79 *From Dread in the Eyes of Horses*

80 *Death of the Horses by Fire*

82 *The Cloudy Shoulders of the Horses*

83 *Legacy*

85 *Gray Eyes*

87 *Woodcutting on Lost Mountain*

I

SUDDEN JOURNEY

Maybe I'm seven in the open field—
the straw-grass so high
only the top of my head makes a curve
of brown in the yellow. Rain then.
First a little. A few drops on my
wrist, the right wrist. More rain.
My shoulders, my chin. Until I'm looking up
to let my eyes take the bliss.
I open my face. Let the teeth show. I
pull my shirt down past the collar-bones.
I'm still a boy under my breast spots.
I can drink anywhere. The rain. My
skin shattering. Up suddenly, needing
to gulp, turning with my tongue, my arms out
running, running in the hard, cold plenitude
of all those who reach earth by falling.

BIRD–WINDOW–FLYING

If we had been given names to love
each other by, I would take this one
from you, bird flying all day
in my woodhouse. The door
is open as when you came
to it, into it, as space between branches. "Never
trust doors," you tell the window,
the small of your body flung
against the white bay.

At dusk when I walked in
with my armload of green alder
I could see the memory of light
shining water through your wings. You
were gray with it. The window
had aged you with promises.
I thought the boats, the gulls
should have stilled you
by now. When I cupped

my hands in their shadows, warm
over the heartwings, I saw the skin
of light between my fingers
haloed and glowing. Three steps I
took with you, for
you, three light years traveling
to your sky, beak
and claw of you, the soft burr of flight
at my fingerbones.

If I take a lover for every tree, I
will not have again such an opening as
when you flew from me.

4

I have gone in to build my fire. All
the walls, all the
wings of my house are burning. The flames
of me, the long hair
unbraiding.

UNSTEADY YELLOW

I went to the field to break
and to bury my precious things.
I went to the field
with a sack and a spade,
to the cool field alone.

All that he gave me
I dashed and I covered.
The glass horse, the necklace,
the live bird with its song, with
its wings like two harps—
in the ground, in the damp ground.

Its song, when I snatched it again
to air, flung it with light
over the tall new corn, its pure joy
must have reached him.

In a day it was back, my freed bird
was back. Oh now, what will I do,
what will I do with its song
on my shoulder, with its heart
on my shoulder when we come to
the field, to the high yellow field?

NOT THERE

One whistle, a short husky breath—
like a child blowing into a metal pipe then
listening. The house shudders
as the train passes on the hillside.
Days, mornings—whatever I'm doing I stop
and rush to wave it by. But always
I'm too late for the engineer.
It's the man in the caboose
who's searched out my doorway.
His grave face and hand say *hello-goodbye*—

Other times the train is coming
and I don't go out. I go on
doing what I'm doing—reading, or staring
at the gulls rising and falling above
the waves. I don't
go out. A weight pulls
against the house. I think of his grave face
looking down at the house, of the woman
in the doorway. I don't go out and
I don't go out. These
are the moments when we meet.

BLACK SHIPS

I saw it was no good, that she
had taken him, had made a place of him
in her mind. We leaned together
in the yard in the rain-shattered spill
of roses and I remembered a friend
I'd stopped knowing, her rule
not to decide important matters
after dark—"Wait until morning, things
look different in daylight."

The ring on his finger matched mine. It
rocked on the bone, held
a moment, then slipped
the knuckle. Like a vow
in reverse he
pulled my gold band away.

Did we meet again in daylight? Did stars
pause in their journeys? Were we
two black ships, flags black, black
our hope and blacker still
the way forward alone? Years later
did one come ashore—cargo
of darkness, cargo of salt and honey?

No, neither came again. Daylight
and the harm spoken. Daylight
with a world to do, loving
after love, crossing into a parking lot

with a multitude of inexhaustible stars
making a black wake behind a woman
with no name, but called by name—
White Bird, that flew once, but not again
into the bell tower when the hour was ripe.

LINOLEUM

for MARK STRAND

There are the few we hear of
like Christ, who, with divine grace,
made goodness look easy, had
a following to draw near, gave up
the right things and saw to it
that sinners got listened to.
Sharpening my failures, I remember
the Jains, the gentle swoosh
of their brooms on a dirt path
trodden by children and goats, each
thoughtful step taken in peril of
an ant's life or a fat grub hidden
under a stick. In the car-wash,
thinking of yogis under a tree
plucking hair by hair the head
of an initiate, I feel at least
elsewhere those able for holiness—
its signs and rigors—are at work.
Ignominiously, I am here, brushes
clamped, soap and water pulsing
against my car. (A good sign too,
those asylums for old and diseased
animals.) My car is clean
and no one has had to
lift a finger. The dead
bugs have been gushed away into a soup
of grit and foam—the evidence
not subterranean, but streaming along
the asphalt in sunlight so dazzling
I attend the birth-moment of
the word *Hosannah*!

I care about the bugs and not
in this life will I do enough towards
my own worth in the memory
of them. I appreciate the Jains,
their atonements for my neglect,
though I understand it makes poor farmers
of them, and good we all
don't aspire to such purity so
there's somebody heartless enough to
plow the spuds.

Early on in admiration, I put off
knowledge, and so delayed reading about
the Jains—not to lose
solace. But in the County Library,
turning a page, I meet them as
the wealthiest moneylenders
in Western India. Reading on,
I'm encouraged—the list of virtues
exceeds vices—just four
of those: anger, pride, illusion and
greed. The emphasis clearly on
striving. I write them down
in the corner of a map
of Idaho: forbearance, indulgence,
straightforwardness, purity,
veracity, restraint, freedom from
attachment to anything, poverty
and chastity.

Choosing, getting into the car to
get to the supermarket, hearing
over engine noise the bright agonies

II

of birds, the radio news with the child
nailed into a broom-closet for
twenty-four hours by parents who
in straightforwardness sacrificed
forbearance, I feel a longing
for religion, for doctrine swift
as a broom to keep the path
clear. Later, alone in the kitchen
with the groceries, I read the list
again. Overwhelmed by the loneliness
of the saints, I take up my broom
and begin where I stand,
with linoleum.

IN THAT TIME
WHEN IT WAS NOT THE FASHION

When the daughters came for me
with their hands webbed in each other's hair,
when they saw, even to the last, how desire
kept me ripe, they grew tender
as the portraits of swans
whose necks are threaded on the open
pond. Their arms at my waist
were strong, were yearning.

We walked near the water's edge.
I told them the one story I called
my life as it began
when I looked back in that far place.

On the table in the land of hunters,
I said, there was meat
and it was eaten. I was born there
with brothers. They learned the ways
of the fathers, could take animals
unawares. Some with their bows
left many days and came to the fire
miraculous, the white deer
on their arrows carrying them far
into pardon. Others returned the same day
and leaned their guns
in the doorway. They were not deceived
about death. The elk hung
their golden heads in the dirt
of the shed. A long suddenness had
closed their eyes open. I
was a child with other children. We
crept up. Our house

had been blessed. We touched
the cold fur, the bald eyes.

My teeth were sharp. I could see the shape
of a leaf in the dark. In one bed
we slept and in the night
we held each other without words or
desire, my brothers now with wives.
Nearest blood that they were, my
changes drove them from me.
My hair was a veil at my back to catch
what looks would follow.

A tall man came into my life. He
liked to dance and be sung to. "Bend
to me," I said, "but not
too far. I like
to reach up." In a time
when it was not the fashion, I neglected
every good chance to live for myself
alone. "What
do you need?" I said. "What pleases
you?"

Even to those unfaithful, at some ripe
moment, I could refuse them
nothing. I sent letters
absolving what hurt they might fear
to have done me. I pledged, I
said, "You are remembered well."
When they brought their new, their old
loves to meet me, I embraced them, I
let my picture be taken in their company.

I learned, in short, to stand with them
in the beloved past moments
so that nothing might be lost.

I would give you hope
against all this if I could.
But I cannot. I have drunk insects
at night from the river. Nor
did I wait for the fruit to fall.
I walked without thinking who lives
in the ground, too many steps. Not even
my death will have me. I am old
and unfinished. Keep watch for me.
I will have children to give away.

THE SHIRTS

They would be shamed to see back at us,
themselves among the others.
I have done this, have hung them
side by side. Did I ask this
or did they come to me? And what
can it mean that I keep their shapes
without them?

They are all colors and one
has thin stripes with lavender. My hands
from the sleeves are another's, reminding,
and the small, exact musculature
of his arms takes on my body.
When I left he said, "Take this. Until
I see you next." Much later
he would tell her name, the woman
who bought it. Its changed face
where my breasts force out
and the one thought: our size, the same.

The green one like the moss-light
of lovers on the forest floor, its
shoulders too broad, the collar sharp
with intention. Flannel, the fur
of winter, fires that light up the forehead
and cast the eyes in shadow. In it,
I am the young girl whose protector
fills her with dread and does not
return. Its caution: "Don't
wear this when you meet her."

This one is blue and the man of it
had eyes like that. "Blue," I said,

"send me some good books. I
want to know how you think."
He had a lot of shirts like this one.
When I took it, he could not
miss it as the special one.

Only this have I given back.
The red one. The one with the blotch
of pitch that would not wash out.
Fire-shirt of the question: will it end?
Man with the passion to burn his love out
in me, nightly, daily, the white-hot
tongs of love. He wears it to breakfast.
Wants pure maple syrup. He likes the pitcher
full. He can stand the sweetness.

PAINTED STEPS

I was coming down the wide, painted steps.
I wanted to go with you
in your leaving, the way a farmer would go
behind his horse
to keep the rows straight. Even
when we reached the car door and I knew
the field would not get there in time,
I thought surely he'll find a way
to walk from this so I can see him harmed
and unsure like a man
who would turn back if
he could, if the field were not coming
late under its flock of birds.

The last moments when you leaned
from the car, even then
I thought if only we could believe this
as never, the field would have mercy, would
come down around us like a fine, healing
rain. I stood where the car had been
and looked out as far as I could, believing
so the light would deepen
and drop off, the field
empty and settle one patch of sky.

But no, I'm not one of those
who changes an ending to keep the moment true.
Think of me as one who lives things quickly,
cruelly as a car could live it.
Think of me as one who stands in the streets,
speeding past with the stopped wheel
in my hands, and the radio, its small hearth
flickering along the trees ahead.

YOU TALK ON YOUR TELEPHONE;
I TALK ON MINE

If you had flown here in a jet
we couldn't be closer, farther. Yes, sit
down. I'm like this often with myself,
waiting to be asked by someone not here into
chairs and cupboards. I can't see
yours, but would offend them daily with
loving. Just to be around
opening and shutting. Let's pick up

where we left off. What were we meaning
the last time I didn't see you?
Are they filming this? I mean you
putting your mouth to the receiver
personably. I'm doing it too, naturally,
out here in my cabin on the bay. Lots
of windows to let in water, weeds
sitting around drying up in mason jars.
All that woodsy romance. I just walked

over to the window. You had no idea I bet,
I was moving around during that last
sentence. Or did I sound restless?
That word bringing my sleep up, how the ocean
kept making for the house all night.
Of course I like your voice. Do you like
mine? That is, do I sound like me in-person?
With clothes on or without? Put on
a little nakedness in what you just said, will
you? It's hard to know what to look

at when you say those things. Sight
can be inappropriate, even missing altogether

when two voices hook-up across the miles.
Just now, we could both be blind and not feel
handicapped by inattentiveness or
groping across the coffee table. You
could be hearing me like birth, the most
important pain and joy in the room. Not
knowing for sure, I can think of you

cave-like where some Indian built
fires once and sat there in his smoke
sharpening a stick with a stone. Elemental.
Though this Africa, dear Watson, keeps growing.
Who can depend on coincidences anymore to give
significance, meeting head-on in jungles
with wild beasts eyeing so our bodies
turn edible, causing the spirits in us to push

civil into friendly, shaking hands like
shaking ghosts. Please, tell me that same joke
twice so I know it's you. Your laughing first
helps with my suspense. Somewhere, no doubt,
they are preparing a nice kettle
for us, these natives, full of sly jubilations,
anxious to dress up in our clothes and meet
the next planetary shipwreck in gabardine
or plumes. How should they know, only
visitors are in style?

Having said all this, if I were to hang up
and call you back, it would still be us, right?
In college days they tried to mess us up
on that one. It creeps in, even now.
I guess because I knew you so long ago

you're always speaking as "back
then." Which is like the Africa
of our childhoods, tigers chasing their tails
around the butter-tree. Africa,
we found out later, was India.

Are they charging us for this or are you
at the office? Your tone is leisurely
with my view of mountains. Sometime
at night I want you to run out
to a phone booth near an all-night gas station
and put the money in. So I can hear it
clink. The distance a little sharper.
Like a glass coffin standing upright
in the dark, a light going on, warm yellow, a body
moving in speech, restless near the pumps.

CONVERSATION WITH A FIREMAN
FROM BROOKLYN

He offers, between planes,
to buy me a drink. I've never talked
to a fireman before, not one from Brooklyn
anyway. Okay. Fine, I say. Somehow
the subject is bound to come up, women
firefighters, and since I'm
a woman and he's a fireman, between
the two of us, we know something
about this subject. Already
he's telling me he doesn't mind
women firefighters, but what
they look like
after fighting a fire, well
they lose all respect. He's sorry, but
he looks at them
covered with the cinders of someone's
lost hope, and he feels disgust, he just
wants to turn the hose on them, they
are that sweaty and stinking, just like
him, of course, but not the woman he
wants, you get me? and to come to that—
isn't it too bad, to be despised
for what you do to prove yourself
among men
who want to love you, to love you,
love you.

CRÊPES FLAMBEAU

We are three women eating out
in a place that could be California
or New Jersey but is Texas and our waiter
says his name is Jerry. He is pink
and young, dressed in soft denim
with an embroidered vest and, my friend says,
a nice butt. It's hard not to be intimate
in America where your waiter wants
you to call him Jerry. So why
do you feel sorry for him
standing over the flames
of this dessert?

The little fans of the crêpes are
folding into the juice. The brandy
is aflare in a low blue hush and golden
now and red where he spills
the brown sugar saved
to make our faces wear the sudden burst. We
are all good-looking and older and he
has to please us or try
to. What could go wrong? Too much
brandy? Too little sugar? Fire
falling into our laps, fire
like laughter behind his back, even
when he has done it just right. "Jerry,"
we say, "that was wonderful," for now
he is blushing at us
like a russet young girl. Our lips

are red with fire and juice.
He knows we could go on
eating long into the night until the flames

run down our throats. "Thank you,"
he says, handing us our check, knowing
among the ferns and napkins that he has
pleased us, briefly, like all
good things, dying away
at the only moment, before
we are too happy, too
glad in the pioneer decor: rough boards,
spotted horses in the frame.

I SAVE YOUR COAT, BUT
YOU LOSE IT LATER

It was a coat worth keeping even with
you in no condition to keep track, your mind
important to things you were seeing out
the window. We had changed seats on the bus
so a little breeze could catch
our faces. The coat was back there in a spot
of sunlight, its leather smell
making a halo of invitation around it.

We got off near the planetarium and were
heading for stars. Just to make one eye do
the work of two and bring back ghost-light
was making us forgetful. Then I looked at
you, strange without your coat, which
I knew you loved and had paid
an incredible price for, as if you had tried
to buy something that would make you sorry.

The bus was worrying itself into traffic, its
passengers locked into destinations. I ran
with everyone until they stopped in their
seats. There was your coat, a big interruption
in everybody's destination. When I picked it up,
it scalded my hand like an unbearable red
I saw once on a woman coming toward me.

We had a forty-year reunion right there
on the street, as if the coat
had met us again in its afterlife. We were
that glad, hugging it between us. Then you put
it on and checked yourself in the store-window
wearing yourself those moments to see forgiveness

take your shape, then catching in the light
of those walking through you. I suppose it was
gratitude, your wearing it with telescopes, me
putting my hand in your pocket, pretending to
rob you while you looked for the first time
at four moons of Jupiter.

Some weeks later, you write your coat was
stolen after a long night of drinking and
music. They took all your money. You never
saw it again. I am in a state of mourning
for your coat which traveled with us that while
like a close relative concealing a fatal illness
in a last visit. I remember a heart doctor
who saved a man for ten hours so his wife
disappeared into hope and would not come back
and would not take her lips from his until
they wheeled him away. I make too much of this,
your coat, which, stolen or lost, did not belong
to me, which I never wore.

II

WHAT CATHÁL SAID

"You can sing sweet
        and get the song sung
        but to get to the third dimension
        you have to sing it
        rough, hurt the tune a little. Put
        enough strength to it
        that the notes slip. Then
        something else happens. The song
        gets large."

3 A.M. KITCHEN:
MY FATHER TALKING

For years it was land working me, oil fields,
cotton fields, then I got some land. I
worked it. Them days you could just about
make a living. I was logging.

Then I sent to Missouri. Momma
come out. We got married.
We got some kids. Five kids.
That kept us going.

We bought some land near the water.
It was cheap then. The water
was right there. You just looked out
the window. It never left the window.

I bought a boat. Fourteen footer.
There was fish out there then.
You remember, we used to catch
six, eight fish, clean them right
out in the yard. I could of fished to China.

I quit the woods. One day just
walked out, took off my corks, said that's
it. I went to the docks.
I was driving winch. You had to watch
to see nothing fell out of the sling. If
you killed somebody you'd
never forget it. All
those years I was just working
I was on edge, every day. Just working.

You kids. I could tell you
a lot. But I won't.

It's winter. I play a lot of cards
down at the tavern. Your mother.
I have to think of excuses
to get out of the house. You're
wasting your time, she says. You're wasting
your money.

You don't have no idea, Threasie.
I run out of things
to work for. Hell, why shouldn't I
play cards? Threasie,
some days now I just don't know.

BOAT RIDE

Since my girlhood, in that small boat
we had gone together for salmon
with the town still sleeping and the wake
a white groove in the black water, black
as it is when the gulls are just stirring and
the ships in the harbor are sparked with lights
like the casinos of Lucerne.
That morning my friend had driven an hour
in darkness to go with us, my father
and me. There'd been an all-night party.
My friend's face so tired I thought, *Eskimo-eyes*.
He sighed, as if stretched out
on a couch at the back of his mind.

Getting the bait and tackle. What
about breakfast? No breakfast.
Bad luck to eat breakfast before fishing, but
good luck to take smoked salmon to eat
on the water in full sun. Was my friend's coat
warm enough? The wind can come up.
Loaning him my brother's plaid jacket.

Being early on the water, like getting first
to heaven and looking back through memory
and longing at the town. Talking little, and
with the low, tender part
of our voices; not sentences but
friendlier, as in nodding to one who already
knows what you mean.

Father in his rain-slicker—seaweed green over
his coat, over blue work-shirt, over cream-
colored thermal underwear that makes a white V

at his neck. His mouth open so the breath
doesn't know if it's coming or going—like any
other wave without a shore. His mind
in the no-thought of guiding the boat.
I stare into the water folding
along the bow, *gentian*—the blue with darkness
engraved into its name, so the sound
petals open with mystery.

Motor-sound, a low burbling with a chuckle
revolving in the *smack smack* of the bow
spanking water. *You hear me, but you don't
hear me*, the motor says
to the fish. A few stars
over the mountains above the town.
I think *pigtails*, and that the water under us
is at least as high as those mountains, deep
as the word *cello* whispered under water—
cello, cello until it frees a greeting.

We pass the Coast Guard station, its tower
flashing cranky white lights beside
the barracks where the seamen sleep in
long rows. Past the buoy, its sullen red bell
tilting above water. All this time
without fishing—important to get out of
the harbor before letting the lines
down, not time wasted but time
preparing, which includes invitation and
forgetting, so the self is occupied freely
in idleness.

"Just a boat ride," my father says, squinting
   where sun has edged the sky toward Dungeness
   a hazy mix of violet and pink. "Boat ride?"
I say. "But we want salmon."
"I'll take cod, halibut, old shoes, anything
   that's going," says my friend. "And you'll get
   dogfish," my father says. "There's enough
   dogfish down there to feed all Japan."
He's baiting up, pushing the double hooks
   through the herring. He watches us
   let the lines out. "That's plenty," he says,
   like it's plain this won't come
   to much.

Sitting then, nothing to say for a while,
   poles nodding slightly. My friend, slipping
   a little toward sleep, closes his eyes.
Car lights easing along Ediz Hook, some
   movement in the town, Port of the Angels,
   the angels turning on kitchen lights,
   wood smoke stumbling among scattered hemlock,
   burning up questions, the angels telling
   their children to get up, planning the future
   that is one day long.

"Hand me that coffee bottle, Sis," my father
   says. "Cup of coffee always makes the fish
   bite." Sure enough, as he lifts the cup,
   my pole hesitates, then dips. I brace
   and reel. "Damned dogfish!" my father says,
   throwing his cigarette into the water. "How
   does he know?" my friend asks. "No fight,"
I say. "They swallow the hook down

34

their gullets. You have to cut
the leader."

No sun-flash on silver scales when it
breaks water, but thin-bellied brown, shark-
like, and the yellow-eye insignia
which says: *there will be more of us.*
Dogfish. Swallower of hooks, waster of hopes
and tackle. My father grabs the line, yanks
the fish toward the knife, slashes twice,
gashing the throat and underbelly so
the blood spills over his hand.
"There's one that won't come back," he says.

My friend witnesses without comment or
judgment the death and mutilation
of the dogfish. The sun is up. My friend
is wide awake now. We are all wide
awake. The dogfish floats away, and a tenderness
for my father wells up in me, my father
whom I want my friend to love and who intends,
if he must, as he will, to humor us, to keep
fishing, to be recorded in the annals
of dogfish as a scourge on the nation of
dogfish which has fouled his line, which is
unworthy and which he will single-handedly
wipe out.

When the next fish hits my friend's line
and the reel won't sing, I take out my
Instamatic camera: "That's a beautiful
dogfish!" I say. "I'll tell them in New York
it's a marlin," my friend says. I snap

his picture, the fish held like
a trophy. My father leans out of
the frame, then cuts the line.

In a lull I get him to tell stories,
the one where he's a coal miner in Ottumwa,
Iowa, during the Depression and the boss
tries to send the men into a mine where
a shaft collapsed the day before. "You'll
go down there or I'll run you out of
this town," the boss says. "You don't
have to run me. I'm not just leaving
your town, I'm leaving your whole goddamned
state!" my father says, and he turns
and heads on foot out of the town, some
of the miners with him, hitching from there
to the next work in the next state.

My father knows he was free
back there in 1935 in Ottumwa, Iowa, and he
means you to know you don't have to risk
your life for pay if you can tell the boss to
go to hell and turn your heel. What
he doesn't tell is thirty years on the docks,
not a day missed—working, raising
a family.

I unwrap smoked salmon sandwiches and we bite
into them. It is the last fishing trip
I will have with my father. He
is ready to tell the one about the time
he nearly robbed the Seminole Bank in
Seminole, Oklahoma, but got drunk

instead and fell asleep.
He is going to kill five more dogfish
without remorse; and I am going to
carry a chair outside for him
onto the lawn of the Evergreen Radiation
Center where he will sit and smoke
and neither of us feels like talking, just
his—"The sun feels good."
After treatments, after going back
to my sister's where he plays with her baby—
"There's my gal! Is the Kiss Bank
open?"—in the night, rising up in the dream
of his going to say, "Get my billfold," as if
even his belongings might be pulled into
the vortex of what would come.

We won't catch a single salmon that day.
No strikes even. My friend and I
will share a beer and reminisce in advance
about the wonderful dogfishing we had.
My father wipes blood from his knife
across his knee and doesn't
look up. He believes nothing
will survive of his spirit or body. His god
takes everything and will not be
satisfied, will not be assuaged by the hopes, by
the pitiful half-measures of the living.
If he is remembered, that too
will pass.

It is good then,
to eat salmon on the water, to bait the hook
again, even for dogfish, to stare back at

the shore as one who withholds nothing, who,
in the last of himself, cannot put together
that meaning, and need not, but yields in thought
so peacefully to the stubborn brightness of
light and water: we are awake with him
as if we lay asleep. Good memory,
if you are such a boat, tell me
we did not falter in the vastness
when we walked ashore.

ACCOMPLISHMENT

What not to do for him
was hardest, for the life left in us
argued against his going
like a moon banished in fullness, yet
lingering far into morning, pale
with new light, gradually a view of
mountains, a sea emerging—its prickly
channels and dark shelves
breeding in the violet morning. Ships too,
after a while. Some anchored, others
moving by degree, as if to leave without affront
this harbor, a thin shoal curved like an arm—
ever embracing, ever releasing.

He too was shaped to agreement, the hands
no longer able to hold, at rest
on the handmade coverlet. His tongue
arched forward in the open mouth where breath
on breath he labored, the task beyond all strength
so the body shuddered like a chill
on the hinge of his effort, then rose again.

After a time, we saw the eyes gaze upward
without appeal—eyes without knowing or need
of knowing. Some in the room began to
plead, as if he meant to take them with him,
and they were afraid. A daughter bent near,
calling his name, then gave her own,
firmly, like a dock he might swim or cling to.
The breath eased, then drifted momentarily,
considering or choosing, we did not know.

"At some point we have to let him go."

"I know," she said. "I know."

In the last moments the eyes widened and,
with the little strength left, he
strained upward and toward. "He had to be
looking *at* something. You don't look
at nothing that way." Not
pain, but some sharpening beyond
the visible. Not eagerness or surprise, but
as though he would die in time to intercept
an onrushing world, for which
he had prepared himself
with that dead face.

BLACK SILK

She was cleaning—there is always
that to do—when she found,
at the top of the closet, his old
silk vest. She called me
to look at it, unrolling it carefully
like something live
might fall out. Then we spread it
on the kitchen table and smoothed
the wrinkles down, making our hands
heavy until its shape against Formica
came back and the little tips
that would have pointed to his pockets
lay flat. The buttons were all there.
I held my arms out and she
looped the wide armholes over
them. "That's one thing I never
wanted to be," she said, "a man."
I went into the bathroom to see
how I looked in the sheen and
sadness. Wind chimes
off-key in the alcove. Then her
crying so I stood back in the sink-light
where the porcelain had been staring. Time
to go to her, I thought, with that
other mind, and stood still.

CANDLE, LAMP & FIREFLY

How can I think what thoughts
to have of you with a mind so unready?
What I remember most: you did not want
to go. Then choice slipped from you
like snow from the mountain, so death
could graze you over with the sweet
muzzles of the deer moving up from
the valleys, pausing to stare
down and back toward the town. But you
did not gaze back. Like a cut rose
on the fifth day, you bowed
into yourself and we watched the shell-
shaped petals drop in clumps, then,
like wine, deepen into the white cloth.

What have you written here on my sleep
with flesh so sure I have no choice
but to stare back when your face and
gestures follow me into daylight?
Your arms, too weak at your death
for embracing, closed around me and held,
and such a tenderness was mixed there
with longing that I asked, "Is it good
where you are?"

We echoed a long time in the kiss
that was drinking me—*daughter, daughter,
daughter*—until I was gone as when a sun
drops over the rim of an ocean, gone
yet still there. Then the dampness,
the chill of your body pulled from me
into that space the condemned
look back to after parting.

Between sleep and death
I carry no proof that we met, no proof
but to tell what even I must call dream
and gently dismiss. So does
a bird dismiss one tree for another
and carries each time the flight between
like a thing never done.
And what is proof then, but some trance
to kill the birds? And what are dreams
when the eyes open on similar worlds
and you are dead in my living?

THE KNEELING ONE

I was taking the little needed, not more,
so the earth could carry me, the way
a tree is able for many birds at once if
they are sure to leave and bear themselves
lightly. I was thinking of home, wanting to
go there again, stepping along the roadside
with a branch I had chosen. Came
horses. Came men
on the horses. Their faces
pressed to my neck.

After, I was changed and did not know
how to show it. When they were gone
I started for home. One horse
they left for me, red horse in sunlight,
brown horse in shadow. I knelt
to the horse. I led it beside me.
Where it grazed I slept.

One knee in homage, two in worship—
I worshiped, I paid homage. With
my two lips and my eyes did I kneel.
With my forehead and heart. I did so.
Perhaps at first it was simple entreaty
as among unsophisticated peoples who
wish only to be spared. But gradually,
as I knelt before a tree or river,
I saw it was more, more even than
reverence, this attention
that grew in me.

My knees became callus like a camel's.
My knees did ache and toughen. Not
like the Carthusians who, bending

44

the knee, would not touch earth, did I
kneel, but as Stephen knelt
before his death with those who had
stoned him looking on, knelt on
both knees and, I think, not
in prayer.

All manner of things and beings were
placed in my path—the hooves
of a slain deer, head of a murderer
fresh from the block, a basket of pears.
I am a spirit with many duties and no
masters, I said. I am the kneeling
one, and I knelt to each.
But what do you want? they asked.
It's not out of wanting, I said,
and passed on.

I reached home. I knelt to
the mother, to the womb that had borne
me. At my father's grave I stayed
kneeling as the dusk came down. He
did not speak, but he felt my kneeling,
of this I am certain. It made
a small bright ripple on the minds
of the dead.

A few onlookers followed me
in the blue twilight. Where will you
go now? they wanted to know.
I will go to the house of my childhood,
I said, and there I will kneel
and kneel down for a while.

DEVOTION: THAT IT FLOW;
THAT THERE BE CONCENTRATION

i

My friend keeps kissing me goodbye, the kisses
landing, out of nervousness, on and about
the face. "Leave the mistakes in," Ives told
his conductor, handing him the new score.
So it feels good, these sudden lips jabbing the chin
and forehead. We couldn't repeat it if
we tried. Looking back to him from the train, I'll
wave, though not too long—like a soul heading into
the underworld—but more as one standing at
the beginning of the beginning, a faint
smile, or as with stage fright suffered inexplicably
in an orchard.
                           We're moving.
The card players in the club car look up
as though they could prevent countryside—but we're
slicing into marshland so surely, a river
gives way to hillside, the backs of houses, an iron
fence, the bricks of a factory where paper tubes
are made.
                Light falling into
            me. *Into*. Blades of light. Light
         with its own breath. So fast—the trees,
                           it moves the trees.

The porter has carried my suitcases.
  Now he asks how I want my coffee: "Black," I say,
"black and strong."
"Like me," he says, and it isn't a question.

It is mid-November and the first snow keeps arriving
between the tracks where the landscape stops briefly
at Providence. A bell rings. The iron wheels
shift for us. Snow, audible to the eyes, reconciles
endless variation. The tracks like a blank musical
score, running now beside us where the trees in clumps
dart up their sudden clefts.

> *Who's gone? Who's*
> *gone? Snowheart—where did you, into whose*
> *past go*
> *with only those particles of light*
> *exactly melting?*

I'm drinking coffee as we pass a child's camp—
a hatch of discarded boards. It is perched
like the abandoned nest of some enormous bird,
topping a bluff which carries as memory
into childhood where once we dug a house into
a hillside. The smell of earth fresh around us, dirt
sifting out of our sleeves beside our plates
at supper. We were the dead children, come home
to sit in goodness with the silence of our ghostly
parents. Now we are gone, and so are they, and where
I look up, the child's camp is a thicket the snow
has breathed on.

> Vision shaved away—the cords of my vision
>   electric, sparked in the current of
> fast ditches, fast silos, chimneys that leap and
>   dodge the banks. Water
> standing in yellow grass, leaves, a few
>   left hanging, tortured so
> the words *defoliation* and *napalm* occur.

The opening pages of Malraux's *Lazarus*: mustard gas
drifting over the Russians in their trenches at Bolgako
until the Germans change their minds about killing
those they have already killed, take the dead
and half-living soldiers in their arms and
stumble back to lives never again the same.

> Passing as another kind of dwelling.
> At night the mills are torches between
> the trees. The snow climbs up, floats
> under the blue
> dark. The tunnels
> of the rabbits quiver and loosen when
> the fur rushes through them.

ii

I have traveled like sky with water far below, an
interlocking of surfaces. Or does the water lift
when sky hints into infinity
that change is the only durable ghost? This powder
of moments sheds the difference. Each shift,
eccentric and willful, is recorded as surely as
the chambers of the heart record blood
that will pass again, asking from time to
time where the body is.

> Interior of my face in the window, axis
> with a darkening motion.
> The mind flies out
> into this unconcealing.
> Shadows
> I kissed.

The rutted track of thought without
                    purpose.

We arrive at Mystic, the mind feeling itself as surface
to steeple, lumberyard, old barrels, a newly built
set of steps heading for a second story: "Up!"
my sight says, until a door opens
                    and a child steps out
                                        onto the landing.

                    iii

We pass over trains, then into a conflicting mesh
of wrecked machines. A gull appears like a fish
above an empty playground. Then WALL, its rushing: WALL
inches from my window, the eyes—their flesh
driven back into the body.

How many times we defy matter heading into the ground
until it rises to either side—shoots by as motion
suddenly delivered to hillside or the mind incarnate—
retaining each recent death at its most living point.

Lunch at Old Saybrook.
The elderly woman across from me reads her newspaper
with a magnifying glass. Something blue flashes by.
                    Blue catches
in the landscape for miles.

The woman has spread her coat across her knees.
She is asleep, or seems so. A graveyard near a river
startles no one's composure, though some
who didn't mean to be looking must see it, where,

in its stead, a yellow truck passes to a yellow house
we lose before woods again.

The woman is asleep and I think my seeing keeps
the world for her. I think of her
like a picnic table in winter, passively unanchored
by the season. I see IS
under her magnifying glass in the empty seat next to her.

iv

At night the houses flicker
between the trees. Every light is the same face you
cannot leave, saying: "I am not leaving,
though I kiss the last mouth, yours, even
yours, without touching."

My eye roars its black blood across the snow-light. My
lantern swings me in a golden arc.
Show-me-show-me: the dwarf flowers
of their heads
in the windows, in the night water.

Bless now
each lit place where no one
will pass tonight, these yellow shrines, elbows
into the dark.

v

The porter wants to know what I've written.
I read it to him where he stands in the aisle, and
he says, "That's beautiful. Is that

what you do for a living?"
"Yes," I say, "for a living."

We pull into yet another station, and he pats my hand,
leans close. "You're lucky," he says, and I feel
all that has gotten away from me
in what he misses. When I step down
onto the platform, there is a train in my memory.
Memory which rushes to add itself
to the startling impression of future pouring in.

The sleeping woman stays with the train, sleeping on,
grave and constant as the silent towns arrive.

VIEW FROM AN EMPTY CHAIR

Late afternoon light between peach trees.
No movement. Just one child-voice
telling another, "I'll show you!"—then
heading into valor—sound of furious pedaling,
clash of spokes. A wash of sparrows
breathes from a rooftop where periscopes
of pipes and ducts cause the houses
to submerge in the deep air.

Behind me, the muzzle of a hound
snuffles the stone ledge. Mournfully, I
occur to him, an intonation of wrongness
in the landscape. I feel the danger I mean
to someone unknown and near.

Over the wall a coffee mug appears, then
upper torso. The woman lets the dog
bound against her. "He hates
men," she tells me. His soft, loose mouth
lunges against the guard-wire—proving
loyalty by insistence on threat.

She lives alone, has had tools
stolen from the patio. Visitors and
burglars chance the house-dog, a terrier
I hear as *terror*. (The air
is finely tuned.) One glance away
and her head is gone.

Country-western bleeds from a doorway
opened brightly to *there goes my
everything*, then shut so birds
come in as underscoring to a car

luffing past. My house, with quiet skill,
intends to pull over me
with shadow.

The child recurs, imitating death pains
as comic and reversible. Taking up
my sweater and waterglass, I catch hold
of a child's drawing the wind has carried
into the yard. It has a friendly aspect,
the mouth like a hammock, though the hands
are levers and the eyes—demented
and aslant. We brighten once before
the house drops over us.

I TAKE CARE OF YOU: A LANTERN
DASHES BY IN THE GRASS

for my sister, STEVIE

Already there is a rhythm to keep.
I bring you your face cloth, steaming.
I prop your leg with pillows
and pull the bright afghan over you.
The woman next to you in the hospital
still speaks though we have left her
for home. "They bring me flowers, but
no hairbrush. My friends—what
do they know, there in their houses?"

I bring you your hairbrush. Your
hair hangs over the back
of the chair, its
waterfall, the first half-way glance
from the cliff. When I brush, it
falls and falls.

You are my good pony. I braid
every fine hair so your neck shows proud
to advantage. They are coming to
see you. Your eyes prance
about the room. You take the mirror
from the tray and the flowers flash up
around your face. Behind you, I
recede to a patch of wallpaper
from our childhood, put on askew so
the pony can't line up with his cart. His
blinders are flared. His. And he
is noble in his abrupt field
pulling one of the many nautical

54

lanterns. His driver—what confidence
though the horse is missing!—his red
cap, his half-a-face sliced
by a strip of magnolia.

I raise the blind
and a bolt of houses steps towards us
in the shocked light. "Today, today!"
the light says, though the porch bulb
glimmers. A man with a dalmatian
opens the house over your desk. "Hand
me that," you say and I do.

The little pony rages through our lives
dragging its benevolent lantern. "Take me
home," the white-haired woman says. It
is two days ago and we know her home is
a span of hope that has swept her
by. "Lean back," I say. "Drink
this. We are a long way off and covered up.
Someone is coming to see us."

WILLINGLY

When I get up he has been long at work,
his brush limber against the house.
Seeing him on his ladder under the eaves,
I look back on myself asleep in the dream
I could not carry awake. Sleep
inside a house that is being painted,
whole lifetimes now only the familiar cast
of morning light over the prayer plant.
This "not remembering" is something new
of where you have been.

What was settled or unsettled in sleep
stays there. But your house
under his steady arm is leaving itself
and you see this gradual surface of
new light covering your sleep
has the greater power.
You think now you felt brush strokes or
the space between them, a motion
bearing down on you—an accumulation
of stars, each night of them
arranging over the roofs of entire cities.

His careful strokes whiten the web,
the swirl of woodgrain blotted
out like a breath stopped
at the heart. Nothing has changed
you say, faithlessly. But something has
cleansed you past recognition. When
you stand near his ladder looking up
he does not acknowledge you,
and as from daylight in a dream you see
your house has passed from you
into the blessed hands of others.

This is ownership, you think, arriving
in the heady afterlife of paint smell.
A deep opening goes on in you.
Some paint has dropped onto your shoulder
as though light concealed an unsuspected
weight. You think it has fallen through
you. You think you have agreed to this,
what has been done with your life, willingly.

STOPPING PLACE

for SHAWN

In those other rooms we may not be
so favored, and if
the man in the green lab coat enters,
at least we have met him in hallways
enough times to stay ahead of
what he may do, actually: the way
we recognize a mermaid,
having studied fish, and women who swim
with their breasts showing.

The space we breathe in is a blink
in the sun. We start our engines and
go. For someone else, it's
over, like the twenty-year-old man
in the cancer ward, found with his book
opened to "Career Opportunities," his pulse
shut for good.

My engine wants to leave the book open too—
or to close it in
with distance, like the Japanese poet, Mutso
Takahashi, who said, "Untalented and
ignorant as I am, I wish
to 'pursue poetry'
at least until I'm eighty-five."

Reading him, even in translation, is
to stroke open the eyes
of a dove. You want to fly for it, or
to speak with feathers. Its wings
glint over the waters—opening, closing, as
one slow silhouette of breath
empties back.

SOME WITH WINGS, SOME WITH MANES

Over the stone wall her hand comes,
each knuckle enlarged to a miniature
skull. She reaches into my rented yard
to call me neighbor. Sunlight dazzles
her spectacles and in the chromium glint
of her walker, she is bright royalty
on an errand of magnitude. An effort to
stand, an effort to step the pain
carefully around invisible parameters
and still to say: effort is nobility.

Her hands are perfectly good for pointing.
That small, bare tree near my walkway, if
pruned, would be heavy with peaches
the size of your fist by July. In new regard,
I think what it could and will do. Then, not
to demean its offering, keep the next thought—
that I'll be gone by summer.

She has the name of a workhorse
I knew in Missouri, Dolly, and has outlived
a sister lost to the same disease. "She
sat down with it and that was the end of
her." Such variations on reluctance
cause me to see a kite
stubborn in a childhood pear tree, still abash
in the wind with its complication
of branches. I sighted my days
by its banners, until the tree caressed it
into flight, one day I wasn't looking.

For didn't the memory of the tree go with
it, the shred of it, less articulate

by then, a slip of motion longing to wrap itself
in a tattered lunge at the whole air?
After that, the tree said only the same thing
other trees say before coming to fruit.
Somehow we knew in our child-hearts
when a thing is ruined, not to meddle
with ecstasy by setting it free. We left it,
though it ruffles the mind yet.

Sitting in the darkened afternoon of her
living room, I hear the death
of the only daughter, meet the husband
who loves eggs and sweets, says little.
"I'm the last of my family," she says, then,
in the walker, leads me down the grassy corridor
to a room sleeping like a princess. The spell,
I see, is in the elaborate coverlet.

She will teach me how to do it. "It
took me fourteen months of evenings,"
the hands now going out
to the stitched pieces, remembering they
have done this. I know I will never do it,
will be gone by summer. "What is it called?"
"Cathedral Windows," she says,
and the razed light of her hands
falls over me.

SOME PAINFUL BUTTERFLIES
PASS THROUGH

I saw the old Chinese men standing
in Nanjing under the trees where
they had hung their caged birds
in the early morning as though a cage
were only another branch that travels
with us. The bird revolves and settles,
moving its mind up and down the tree
with leaves and light. It sings
with the free birds—what else
can it do? They sit on the rungs
and preen or jit back and down and
back. But they are busy
and a day in the sky makes wings
of them. Then some painful butterflies
pass through.

The old men talk and smoke, examine
each other's cages. They feel restored,
as if they'd given themselves a tree, a sky
full of companions, song
that can travel. They depend
on their birds, and if their love stories
swing from their arms as they walk
homeward, it may be they are chosen
after all like one tree
with one bird that is faithful,
an injured voice traveling high into silence

with one accustomed listener
who smiles and walks slowly with
his face in the distance so
the pleasure spreads, and the treasured
singing, and the little bursts
of flying.

[*Shanghai / June 11, 1983*]

EATING THE SPARROWS

A platter of walnuts, I think.
Shanghai and the banquet is festive.
Strong Chinese brandy and "Campi!"
so we drink to the bottom.
The sparrows drop to my plate, their
tiny drumsticks clamped to their sides,
a nub of wings, a slash of beak. "Eat!"
our host says. My mouth flickers and
swoops in the tall room. Sparrows, why
you should come to me with your
slivers of meat and your songless sky
I don't know. Nor how you fell, by what
blow or trick, what feast of crumbs.
Who asked for your sacrifice? Do
your deaths cross from famine
onto this plentiful island of friendship?
I watch the host, nimble
over the carcass with pleasure. It is time
to pick up your unlucky sparrow, believe
against your safety. Sparrow,
your message is clear: it is not too late
for my singing.

[*Guilin / June 17, 1983*]

III

SKYLIGHTS

In the night I get up and walk
between the slices of deep blue sky.
After a time, I lie down on the floor
and stare up like a child on a roof. Stars
tug at my face. The rooms commune
like hillsides. I think of antelope, of
the talons of owls, of a tiger
that has not eaten for days.
"Come to bed," the man calls to me. "What
are you doing?" The moon
has floated into my coffin.
In a cool, white light I rise
and go downstairs to the kitchen table.
A little starlight clings
to the tablecloth, the clock face, the rim
of a water glass. "Is anything
the matter?" he calls. It is then
the wild sound comes to my throat and
for a moment my house hurtles through space
like the word *hungry*
uttered by an army of tigers
advancing on a column of children.
Stillness. The moon
caresses the carcasses of tigers
and children. I alone am spared.
Softly then, his footsteps.

TABLEAU VIVANT

They think it's easy to be dead, those
who walk the pathway here in stylish shoes,
portable radios strapped to their arms,
selling the world's perishables, even
love songs. They think you just lie down
into dreams you will never tell anyone.
They don't know we still have plans, a yen
for romance, and miss things like hats
and casseroles.

As for dreams, we take up where the living
leave off. We like especially those
in which the dreamer is about to
fall over a cliff or from a bridge that
is falling too. We're only too glad
to look down on the river gorge enlarging
under a body's sudden weight, to have the ground
rushing up instead of this slow
caving in. We thrive on living out
the last precious memories of someone escaped
back into morning light.

Occasionally there's a message saying they want
one of us back, someone out there
feeling guilty about a word or deed
that seems worse because we took it as
a living harm, then died
with it, quietly. But we know a lot about
forgiveness and we always make these trips with
a certain missionary zeal. We get back
into our old sad clothes. We stand again
at the parting, full of wronged tenderness and
needing a shave or a hairdo. We tell them

things are okay, not to waste their lives
in remorse, we never held it
against them, so much happens that no one means.

But sometimes one of us gets stubborn, thinks
of evening the score. We leave them calling
after us, *Sorry, Sorry, Sorry*, and we don't
look back.

THE HUG

A woman is reading a poem on the street
and another woman stops to listen. We stop too,
with our arms around each other. The poem
is being read and listened to out here
in the open. Behind us
no one is entering or leaving the houses.

Suddenly a hug comes over me and I'm
giving it to you, like a variable star shooting light
off to make itself comfortable, then
subsiding. I finish but keep on holding
you. A man walks up to us and we know he hasn't
come out of nowhere, but if he could, he
would have. He looks homeless because of how
he needs. "Can I have one of those?" he asks you,
and I feel you nod. I'm surprised,
surprised you don't tell him how
it is—that I'm yours, only
yours, etc., exclusive as a nose to
its face. Love—that's what we're talking about, love
that nabs you with "for me
only" and holds on.

So I walk over to him and put my
arms around him and try to
hug him like I mean it. He's got an overcoat on
so thick I can't feel
him past it. I'm starting the hug
and thinking, "How big a hug is this supposed to be?
How long shall I hold this hug?" Already
we could be eternal, his arms falling over my
shoulders, my hands not
meeting behind his back, he is so big!

I put my head into his chest and snuggle
in. I lean into him. I lean my blood and my wishes
into him. He stands for it. This is his
and he's starting to give it back so well I know he's
getting it. This hug. So truly, so tenderly
we stop having arms and I don't know if
my lover has walked away or what, or
if the woman is still reading the poem, or the houses—
what about them?—the houses.

Clearly, a little permission is a dangerous thing.
But when you hug someone you want it
to be a masterpiece of connection, the way the button
on his coat will leave the imprint of
a planet in my cheek
when I walk away. When I try to find some place
to go back to.

READING ALOUD

When the light was shutting down on you
I said, "Behind my home is a palace of mountains."
I wanted you to see them, regal
in their shawls of snow above the working houses
of the town. I told them to you
the way a mother tells death to a child, so it seems
possible to go there and stay, leaving everyone
behind, saying softly, "Everyone's coming,"
so it's only a little while alone.

You were slipping from our days
like an opposite ripeness, still clinging
to the light. Each time you guessed your way home
by the edges, I saw my own image
freed in the streets of your memory, my face
like a time-traveler's, forever young,
and every place you touched gave way.

I called it my year of the blind.
I was working for your friend who lived
a blindness he was born to.
"What did he lose? Noises, that's all
he knows," you said, would have no comfort
or instruction.

Long days I read aloud to your friend
the words that are the fountain sounds of the mind
causing light to fall inside itself over
the missing shapes of the world. "What do you think
when I say 'wings'?" I asked once. "Angels,
birds," he said, and I saw he could fly
with either. Once about diamonds,

"Their light—a hiss in the rain
when the cars pass."

But you were memory-taunted by what was left
of your sight—the face of a beautiful
gradeschool teacher marooned in your childhood.
You cried against her neck and were grown.

The day we set out for the mountains
I strapped your sleeping bag to your back.
The woman who would call you "husband"
bound up her long hair and said your name
each time you fell and got up, *David, David*.
When we came to the chasm where a moss-slick log
was the only bridge, we looked down for you
at the river-stones, the water over
and over them.

She loved you too much and could not lead you.
I took your hand and put all my sight there,
balancing between trust and the swiftness
we could fall to, walking backwards
so my grip was steady. When the river-sound
rocked us to either side, I fell deeper
for how you gave up to me
and to the river where we walked
like two improbable Christs held up by the doubt
that is the body.
When I let your hand drop on the far side
and we sank in the earth, the habit
of thanks was in me. Who could go with us
after that, though they joined us?

When I think of you in the years that have
passed us, I see a river under you
and always you are walking
into the shouting light of water and again
the wet smell of cloth
as when someone has been lifted free
with their breath still in them.

I know your walking is the other side of courage
and has no regard, like the cold faces
of the mountains, seen from a childhood window
when the house is empty, when
with our many hands we have rushed through the rooms,
adding darkness, adding the words *mother, father,*
and no one answers back.

UNANSWERED LETTER

Your silence is leaning toward judgment.
Yesterday I bragged, writing to calm
my paranoid friend, that I never assume
the worst when my pals don't write. Now
assuming the worst, I think what I must have
done, or not done. Surely some recognition
will brand the door of my house, or
rich attention flutter down.

How natural, in silence, to credit delay
with intention, like the word *oar*
insisting on water. The need also to
advise the self around exaggeration,
i.e., "nobody loves me," because nothing *is*
coming back, and, next to nothing, not
to act like a transistor radio left on into
the night, voices singing like an ear
baffled by the rain, or someone refused
because they think so.

Those others you loved elsewhere, you miss
what they haven't said. They belong
to some permission to go on as more
than yourself, a clarity that adds you back
to all you cast off, as when
you want to be the good light of a lamp
scanning the firmament, or rain—its pleasure
with an open boat.

So what is unanswered keeps you coming back
to yourself, telling you what you wanted
only when it didn't come, having now

to make up this difference.
Even moments you think empty, the world
doesn't stop speaking—the windshield
blurred suddenly by a sighting of gravestones,
before you are driven
                    through the underpass.

EACH BIRD WALKING

Not while, but long after he had told me,
I thought of him, washing his mother, his
bending over the bed and taking back
the covers. There was a basin of water
and he dipped a washrag in and
out of the basin, the rag
dripping a little onto the sheet as he
turned from the bedside to the nightstand
and back, there being no place

on her body he shouldn't touch because
he had to and she helped him, moving
the little she could, lifting so he could
wipe under her arms, a dipping motion
in the hollow. Then working up from
the feet, around the ankles, over the
knees. And this last, opening
her thighs and running the rag firmly
and with the cleaning thought
up through her crotch, between the lips,
over the V of thin hairs—

as though he were a mother
who had the excuse of cleaning to touch
with love and indifference
the secret parts of her child, to graze
the sleepy sexlessness in its waiting
to find out what to do for the sake
of the body, for the sake of what only
the body can do for itself.

So his hand, softly at the place
of his birth-light. And she, eyes deepened

and closed in the dim room.
And because he told me her death as
important to his being with her,
I could love him another way. Not
of the body alone, or of its making,
but carried in the white spires of trembling
until what spirit, what breath we were
was shaken from us. Small then,
the word *holy*.

He turned her on her stomach
and washed the blades of her shoulders, the
small of her back. "That's good," she said,
"that's enough."

On our lips that morning, the tart juice
of the mothers, so strong in remembrance, no
asking, no giving, and what you said, this
being the end of our loving, so as not to hurt
the closer one to you, made me look
to see what was left of us
with our sex taken away. "Tell me," I said,
"something I can't forget." Then the story of
your mother, and when you finished
I said, "That's good, that's enough."

FROM DREAD IN THE EYES OF HORSES

Eggs. Dates and camel's milk.
Give this. In one hour the foal will
stand, in two will run. The care then of
women, the schooling from fear, clamor
of household, a prospect of saddles.

They kneel to it, folded
on its four perfect legs, stroke
the good back, the muscles bunched at the chest.
Its head, how the will shines large in it
as what may be used to overcome it.

The women of the horses comb out
their cruel histories of hair only for
the pleasure of horses, for the lost mares
on the Ridge of Yellow Horses, their white arms
praying the hair down breasts ordinary

as knees. The extent of their power,
this intimation of sexual wealth. From dread
in the eyes of horses are taken their songs.
In the white forests the last free horses
eat branches and roots, are hunted like deer
and carry no one.

A wedge of light where the doorway opens
the room—in it, a sickness of sleep.
The arms of the women, their coarse
white hair. In a bank of sunlight, a man
whitewashes the house he owns—no shores, no
worlds above it and farther, shrill, obsidian,
the high feasting of the horses.

DEATH OF THE HORSES BY FIRE

We have seen a house in the sleeping town
stand still for a fire and the others,
where their windows knew it,
clothed in the remnants of a dream
happening outside them. We have seen
the one door aflame in the many windows,
the steady procession of the houses
trembling in heat-light, their well-tended
yards, the trellis of cabbage roses scrawled
against the porch—flickering white, whiter
where a darkness breathes back.

How many nights the houses have burned through
to morning. We stood in our blankets
like a tribe made to witness
what a god could do.

We saw the house built again in daylight
and children coming from it
as what a house restores to itself in rooms
so bright they do not forget, even
when the father, when the mother
dies. "Kitchen of your childhoods!" we shout
at the old men alive on the benches
in the square. Their good, black eyes
glitter back at us, a star-fall
of homecomings.

Only when the horses began to burn
in the funnel of light hurrying in one place
on the prairie did we begin to suspect
our houses, to doubt at our meals
and pleasures. We gathered on the ridge

above the horses, above the blue smoke
of the grasses, and they whirled in the close
circle of the death that came to them, rippling in
like a deep moon to its water. With
the hills in all directions
they stood in the last of their skies
and called to each other to save them.

THE CLOUDY SHOULDERS
OF THE HORSES

We have thought of our horse, to take
his saddle off so he stands near us
with his back free. His quick skin ripples
with the weight lifted away.
In the brown shallow the minnows
of the flesh go darting.
To be tied by the neck to that
deliberate tree
causes a shift of light
on the river. No, I say, let
the horse drink, let the reins
drag in the flow and the bit
go silver-cold. Let this be called
Slave River.

We raise our heads to see
if the world has waited, we
who that moment were a thought
so unobliged there will be lives
to pay for it, back there
in the city where they are trading shovels
for spoons, a crop
for a day at the wheel.
Spoiled shapes on the water, we drink
from the leaves and wings
above us, from the drifting shoulders
of the horses.

LEGACY

Your eyes close where the horse
flames through the hoop head-on, three
riders totem on its back. One falls
for the crowd-fear of falling; one
thinks of air as a wing broken from her
like bread, like the word *star*
not shining, or the tree—its flight
stopped by a bird.

For the one who stays: motion
and the horse. Together they are
solving the distance—shoulder to arm,
hoof to mane. Borrow this: old
horse, ginger horse, horse amusing your
weakness for him. Garlands we earned
like a handful of flour.

Closer then. Not said. Horse
of our dreams, you carried earth like
a sky. He *was* the victim, even though *he*
said it, a kind of prosperity. "Again"
was not addressed to any woman.
The horse stumbled into his hut. Flames
from it. Shadows with their own bodies.
Once, just watching, he disappeared.
With us, he was less hopeful and meant
funerals just for the sake of ending like
everybody else.

Wounding the horse
was our danger. It wouldn't bleed

until we said goodbye.
The rider felt sorry and got off.
Goodbye, goodbye, we said.
I weighed almost nothing.
In the hut his voice had left
the choir. *I weighed
almost nothing.*

If I mention *you* this is not necessarily
a love poem, though the chance of this
is a conversation you are having
with the horse. Only the birds
keep us from flying. *I weighed
almost nothing.* I have left you
my horse.

GRAY EYES

When she speaks it is like coming onto a grave
        at the edge of a woods, softly, so we
                do not enter or wholly
                turn away. Such speech
        is the breath a brush makes through hair,
                opening into time
                after the stroke.

                A tree is bending
but the bird doesn't land.

                One star,
earthbound, reports a multitude of unyielding
        others. It
                cannot help its   falling   falling
into the dull brown earth of someone's back yard,
        where, in daylight, a hand reaches
in front of the mower and tosses it, dead stone,
                aside. We who saw it fall

are still crashing with light into the housetops,
        tracing in the mind that missing
                trajectory, rainbow of darkness
        where we were—children
murmuring—"There, over there!"—while the houses
        slept and slept on.

Years later she is still nesting on the light
        of that plundered moment, her black hair
                frozen to her head with yearning,
        saying, "Father, I am a colder green
                where the mower cut a swath
                and I lay down

and the birds that have no use for song
        passed over me
   like a shovel-fall."

She closed her eyes. It was early morning. Daybreak.
Some bees
        were dying on my wing—humming
   so you could hardly hear.

WOODCUTTING ON LOST MOUNTAIN

for LESLIE *and for* MORRIS

Our father is three months dead
from lung cancer and you light another Camel,
ease the chainsaw into the log. You
don't need habits to tell us
you're the one most like him.
Maybe the least loved
carries injury farther into tenderness
for having first to pass through
forgiveness. You
passed through. "I think he respected me
at the end," as if you'd waited a lifetime
to offer yourself that in my listening.

"Top of the mountain!" your daughter cries.
She's ten, taking swigs with us
from the beer can in the January sun. We see
other mountain tops and trees forever.
A mountain *could* get lost in all this, right
enough, even standing on it, thinking this
is where you are.

"Remember the cabins we built when we were
kids? The folks logging Deer Park and
Black Diamond." My brother, Morris, nods,
pulls the nose of the saw into the air as a chunk
falls. "We built one good one. They
brought their lunches and sat with us
inside—Spam sandwiches on white bread,
bananas for dessert and Mountain Bars, white
on the inside, pure sugar on
the inside—the way they hurt your teeth."

Sawdust sprays across his knee, his face
closes in thought. "Those whippings." He
cuts the motor, wipes his forehead with an arm.
"They'd have him in jail today. I used to beg
and run circles. You got it worse because you
never cried. It's a wonder we didn't
run away." "Away to where?" I say. "There's no
away when you're a kid. Before you can get there
you're home."

"Once he took you fishing and left me
behind," my brother says.
"I drew pictures of you sinking
all over the chicken house. I gave you a head
but no arms. We
could go back today and there
they'd be, boats
sinking all down the walls."

His daughter is Leslie, named after our father.
Then I think—'She's a logger's daughter,
just like me'—and the thought pleases as if
the past had intended this present. "You
didn't know you were doing it," I tell him,
"but you figured how to stay
in our childhood." "I guess I did. There's
nothing I'd rather do," he says, "than cut wood.
Look at that—" he points to stacks of logs
high as a house he's thinned from the timber—
"they're going to burn them. Afraid
somebody might take a good tree
for firewood, so they'll burn half a forest.
Damn, that's the Forest Service for you. Me—
I work here, they'll have to stop me."

Leslie carries split wood to the tailgate
and I toss it into the truck. We make
a game of it, trying to stack as fast
as her father cuts. "She's a worker,"
Morris says. "Look at that girl go.
Sonofagun, I wouldn't trade four boys for her.
No sir." He picks up the maul, gives a yell
and whacks down through the center of a block
thick as a man. It falls neatly into
halves. "Look at that! Now *that's* good wood.
That's beautiful wood," he says, like he
made it himself.

I tell him how the cells of trees
are like the blood cells of people, how trees
are the oldest organisms on the earth. Before
the English cut the trees off Ireland, the Irish
had three dozen words for green. He's impressed,
mildly, has his own way of thinking about trees.

Tomorrow a log pile will collapse
on him and he will just get out alive.

"Remember the time Dad felled the tree on us
and Momma saved us, pushed us into a ditch? It's
a wonder we ever grew up."

"One of the horses they logged with, Dick
was his name, Old Dick. They gave him
to Oney Brown and Dick got into the house
while everyone was gone and broke
all the dishes. Dishes—what could they mean
to a horse? Still, I think he knew
what he was doing."

Oney's wife, Sarah, had fifteen kids. She's
the prettiest woman I'll ever see. Her son,
Lloyd, took me down to the railroad tracks
to show me the dead hounds. "We had too many
so they had to shoot some." The hounds were
skeletons by then, but they haven't moved
all these years from the memory
of that dark underneath of boughs.
I look at them, stretched on their sides, twin
arches of bones leaping with beetles and
crawlers into the bark-rich earth. Skipper
and Captain—Cappy for short. Their names
and what seemed incomprehensible—a betrayal
which meant those who had care of you
might, without warning, make an end of you
in some godforsaken, heartless place. Lloyd spat
like a father between the tracks, took
my hand and led me back to the others.

Twenty years settles on the boys
of my childhood. Some of them loggers.
"It's gone," they tell me. "The Boom Days
are gone. We thought
they'd never end, there were
that many trees. But it's finished,
or nearly. Nothing but stumps
and fireweed now."

"Alaska," Morris says, "that's where the trees
are," and I think of them, like some lost tribe
of wanderers, their spires and bloodless blood
climbing cathedral-high into the moss-light
of days on all the lost mountains of
our childhoods.

Coming into the town we see the blue smoke
of the trees streaming like a mystery
the houses hold in common.
"Doesn't seem possible—," he says, "a tree
nothing but a haze you could
put your hand through."

"What'll you do next, after the trees are gone?"

"Pack dudes in for elk."

"Then what?"

"Die, I guess. Hell, I don't know, ask
a shoemaker, ask a salmon. . . .
Remember that time I was hunting and got lost,
forgot about the dark and me with no coat, no
compass? You and Dad fired rifles from the road
until I stumbled out. It
was midnight. But I got out. It's a wonder
I could tell an echo from a shot, I was so cold,
so lost. Stop cussing, I told the old man, I'm
home, ain't I? 'You're grown,' he kept saying,
'you're a grown man.'
I must be part wild. I must be part tree or part
deer. I got on the track and I was lost
but it didn't matter. I had to go where it led.
I must be part bobcat."

Leslie is curled under my arm, asleep.

"Truck rocks them to sleep," Morris says.
"Reminds me, I don't have a license for this

piece of junk. I hope I don't get stopped. Look
at her sleep! right in the middle of the day.
Watch this: 'Wake up honey, we're lost. Help me
get home. You went to sleep and got us lost.'
She must be part butterfly, just look at those eyes.
There—she's gone again. I'll have to carry
her into the house. Happens every time.
Watch her, we'll go up the steps and she'll be
wide awake the minute I open the door.
Hard to believe, we had to be carried into houses
once, you and me. It's a wonder we ever
grew up."

Tomorrow a log pile will collapse
and he'll just get out alive.

He opens the door. Her eyes start,
suddenly awake.

"See, what'd I tell you. Wide awake. Butterfly,
you nearly got us lost, sleeping so long.
Here, walk for yourself. We're home."